D1298253

Faucet Fish

Fay Robinson

Illustrated by Wayne Anderson

Dutton Children's Books
New York

CIP Data is available.

Published in the United States 2005 by Dutton Children's Books,
a division of Penguin Young Readers Group
345 Hudson Street, New York, New York 10014
www.penguin.com

Published as *A Fish Wish* in the UK 2005 by The Templar Company plc,
Pippbrook Mill, London Road, Dorking, Surrey RH4 1JE, UK

Manufactured in China

First American Edition

ISBN 0-525-47166-9

2 4 6 8 10 9 7 5 3 1

For Emily, who knew what to do about the whale

F.R.

For Elizabeth Alice

W.A.

Elizabeth loved fish.

She spent every Saturday at the aquarium down the street, drawing her favorite ones. Everyone at the aquarium knew her. The aquarium librarian let her take out all the best books.

The fish feeder let Elizabeth give snails to the octopus. The plumber even let Elizabeth help clean the fish tanks.

At home, Elizabeth had only a guppy. She wanted more than that.

"Mom, can I have a piranha?"

"No, Elizabeth, you may not have a banana. We're eating lunch in just a minute," said Elizabeth's mother.

"Mom, did you hear me? I said I want a piranha. It's a kind of fish. I already have a fishbowl for it."

Elizabeth kept several fishbowls on hand in hopes of using them someday.

"One fish is enough, Elizabeth. Maybe in a few years when you're more responsible."

"Eesh," grumbled Elizabeth.

One day, Elizabeth was washing her hands in the bathroom sink.

Suddenly,

PLUNK!

A trout plopped out of the faucet.

“Oh boy,” said Elizabeth.
She ran to get one of her fishbowls.

“Mom!” Elizabeth called. **“Look! A trout!”**

“Yes, dear,” said her mother.
But she wasn’t listening.

The next day, while Elizabeth brushed her teeth, a flounder flopped out of the faucet.

Elizabeth couldn't believe her luck!

"Dad," said Elizabeth,
"why do flounders have both eyes
on the same side?"

"Elizabeth, show me your project later.
I'm busy now," said Elizabeth's father.

"Nobody **ever** listens to me,"
said Elizabeth.

Elizabeth turned the water on again. Just as she expected, **another** fish appeared.

This one was a little larger than the others and didn't quite fit into any of her fishbowls.

Elizabeth gathered up all the allowance she had been saving and hurried to the pet store. She bought three large fish tanks and hauled them home.

The **next** day,
a moray eel oozed out of the faucet.
A clown triggerfish followed.
Then a squid showed up.

Soon there were tanks full of fish
on every shelf and in every corner—
catfish, dogfish, jellyfish, and rays;
sticklebacks, halibut,
lumpfish, skates...

swishing, zipping, and splashing with delight.

Elizabeth's parents hadn't noticed.

Elizabeth thought she should bring it to their attention.

"I just love having all these fish around," she said at dinner.

"That's nice, dear. Please pass the pepper," said her mother.

Elizabeth tried again. "My favorite fish so far is the sea dragon. Look, it's watching us!"

"Personally, my favorite dish is cauliflower-rutabaga pie. Maybe I'll make one tomorrow," said her father.

After dinner, Elizabeth decided to take a bath. She had just turned on the water when a giant mouth appeared. Elizabeth jumped back and waited while the creature finished squishing through the pipes.

Soon a baby beluga whale **splashed** into the tub.

Elizabeth sighed. "There's no room for any more fish, much less a whale," she said.

"It's time to make my parents listen."

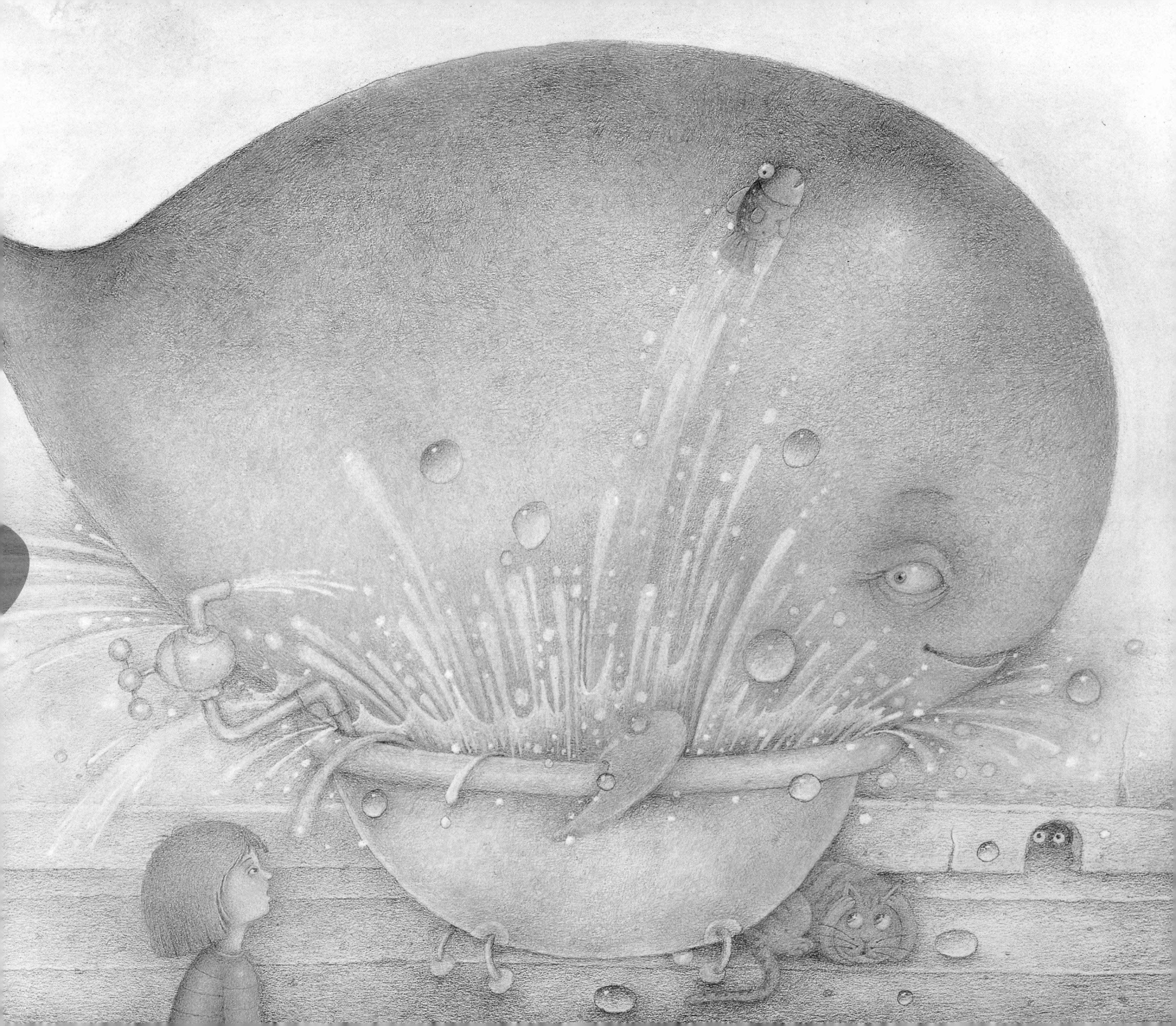

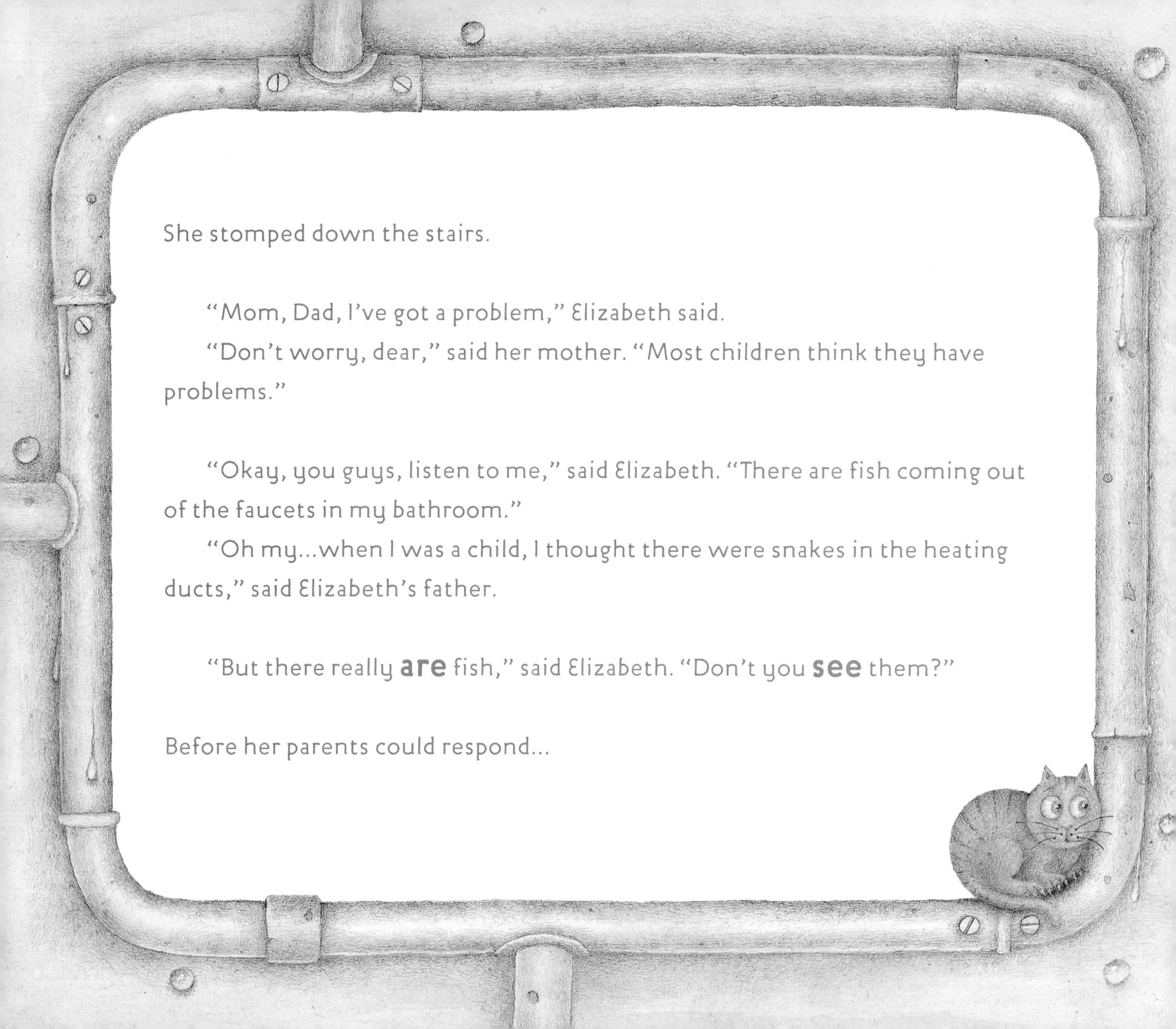

She stomped down the stairs.

"Mom, Dad, I've got a problem," Elizabeth said.

"Don't worry, dear," said her mother. "Most children think they have problems."

"Okay, you guys, listen to me," said Elizabeth. "There are fish coming out of the faucets in my bathroom."

"Oh my...when I was a child, I thought there were snakes in the heating ducts," said Elizabeth's father.

"But there really **are** fish," said Elizabeth. "Don't you **see** them?"

Before her parents could respond...

a rumble from above interrupted them.

“What’s that?” said Elizabeth’s father, looking up.

The ceiling tiles shook and clacked. A trickle of water dribbled onto the kitchen table.

“Is it raining?”

asked Elizabeth’s mother.

A clanging, banging sound came next.
The trickle became a small waterfall.

Ceiling tiles clattered to the floor.
The noise grew thunderous.
"I think we should get out of the way,"
called Elizabeth, pulling her parents to the side.

Suddenly, the ceiling split open as something huge and gray came whooshing down.

crash!!

The beluga whale looked sweetly at Elizabeth's mother from the tub.

"Elizabeth, can you e-e-explain this f-f-fish?" asked Elizabeth's mother.

"It's a beluga whale, Mom."

"Yes, honey, but what's it doing here in our kitchen?"

"It came out of the faucet. It must have been too heavy for the bathroom floor. There are lots of others."

"I've been **trying** to tell you."

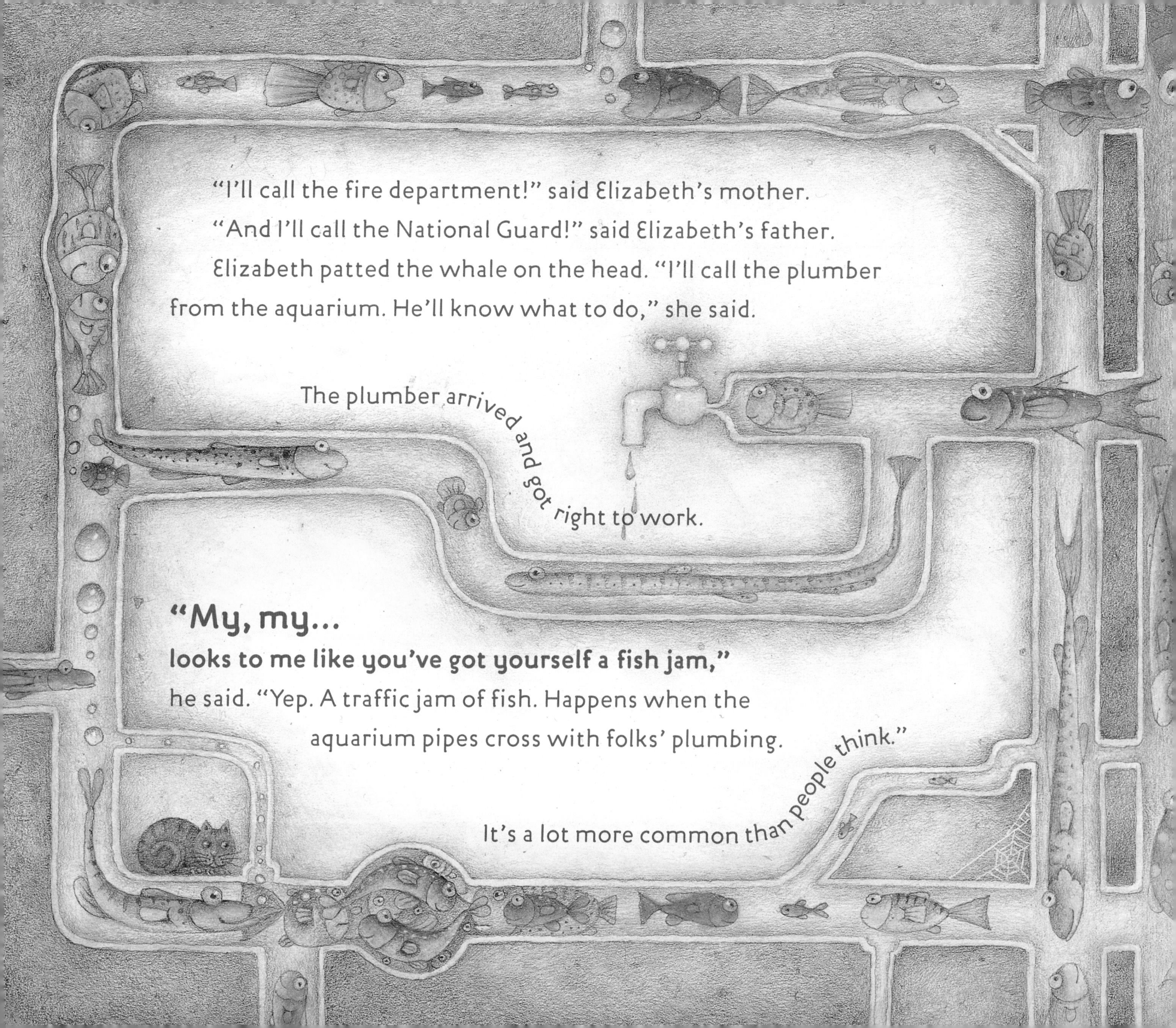

"I'll call the fire department!" said Elizabeth's mother.

"And I'll call the National Guard!" said Elizabeth's father.

Elizabeth patted the whale on the head. "I'll call the plumber from the aquarium. He'll know what to do," she said.

The plumber arrived and got right to work.

"My, my...
looks to me like you've got yourself a fish jam,"
he said. "Yep. A traffic jam of fish. Happens when the aquarium pipes cross with folks' plumbing. It's a lot more common than people think."

"Wha, wha, wha...?" said Elizabeth's mother.
"They don't like being stuck in a pipe
any more than you would," he explained.
"The only thing to do
is to turn on all the faucets and **let 'em out!**"

Elizabeth and the plumber shut all the windows and turned on all the faucets. Then they led everyone outside.

The house filled up with water.

Soon there were fish peering out from every window.

"Might as well turn your house into an aquarium," said the plumber with a wink. "Can't live in it now."

Elizabeth shouted, **"Yes!"**

Her parents gasped.

Elizabeth and her family moved to a house nearby.
Elizabeth's old house became a home for wayward fish. Elizabeth took excellent care of them.

And from then on,
Elizabeth's parents listened **very carefully**
whenever Elizabeth spoke.

Especially when she mentioned a new hobby....